To my grands: Cooper and Lucy and
my progeny: Jim, Mark, John & Steven

JNW

To my niece: Mira Jane

AW

Pepper the Frog
appears on some pages
Ready for Dreams
with friends of all ages

All inquiries to:
James N. West, Skiff Mountain Press
346 East Shore Drive, Whitmore Lake, Michigan 48189, www.jamesnwest.com

Cover Design and Illustrations: Anne Wertheim, www.annewertheim.com

ISBN: 978-1-7343912-2-0 (Hardback)
ISBN: 978-1-7343912-1-3 (Paperback)
Library of Congress Control Number: 2021914195

Dream Time

By James N. West
illustrated by Anne Wertheim

Up with the covers
under the sheet,
head on my pillow
time for sleep!

Ready for bed

teeth are brushed

pajamas have been put on,

let's get settled
let's get comfy
the busy day is done.

Time for dreams
time for rest
time to snuggle so sweet,

head on your pillow
eyes feeling droopy
ready to fall asleep.

Ready for dreams
in your room

as you sleep my little one,
take your rest
sweet child of God
'til the lazy night is done.

Then the sun will rise
rub sleepy eyes

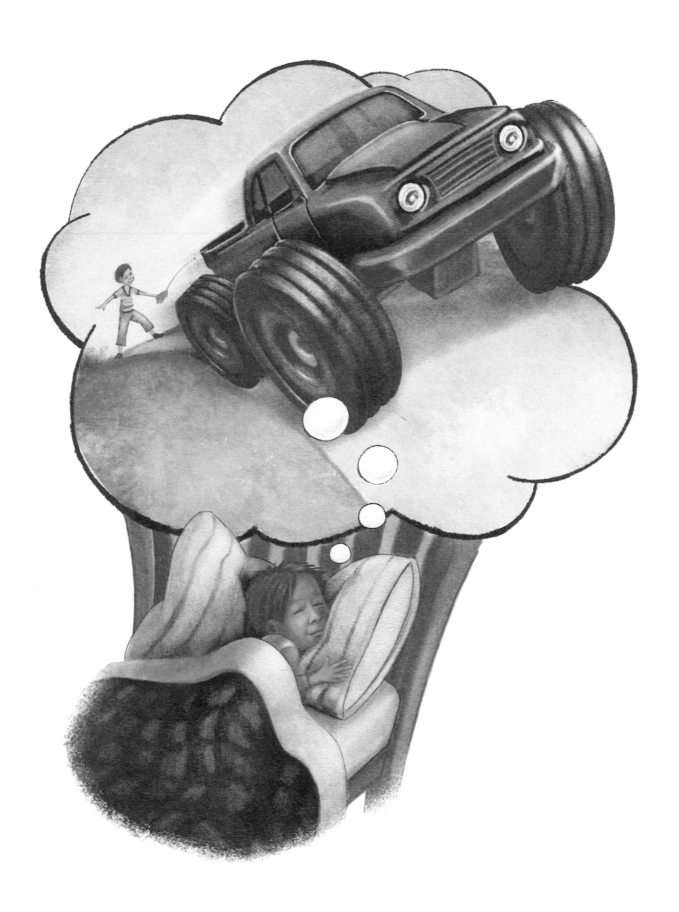

awaken once again,
the brand-new day

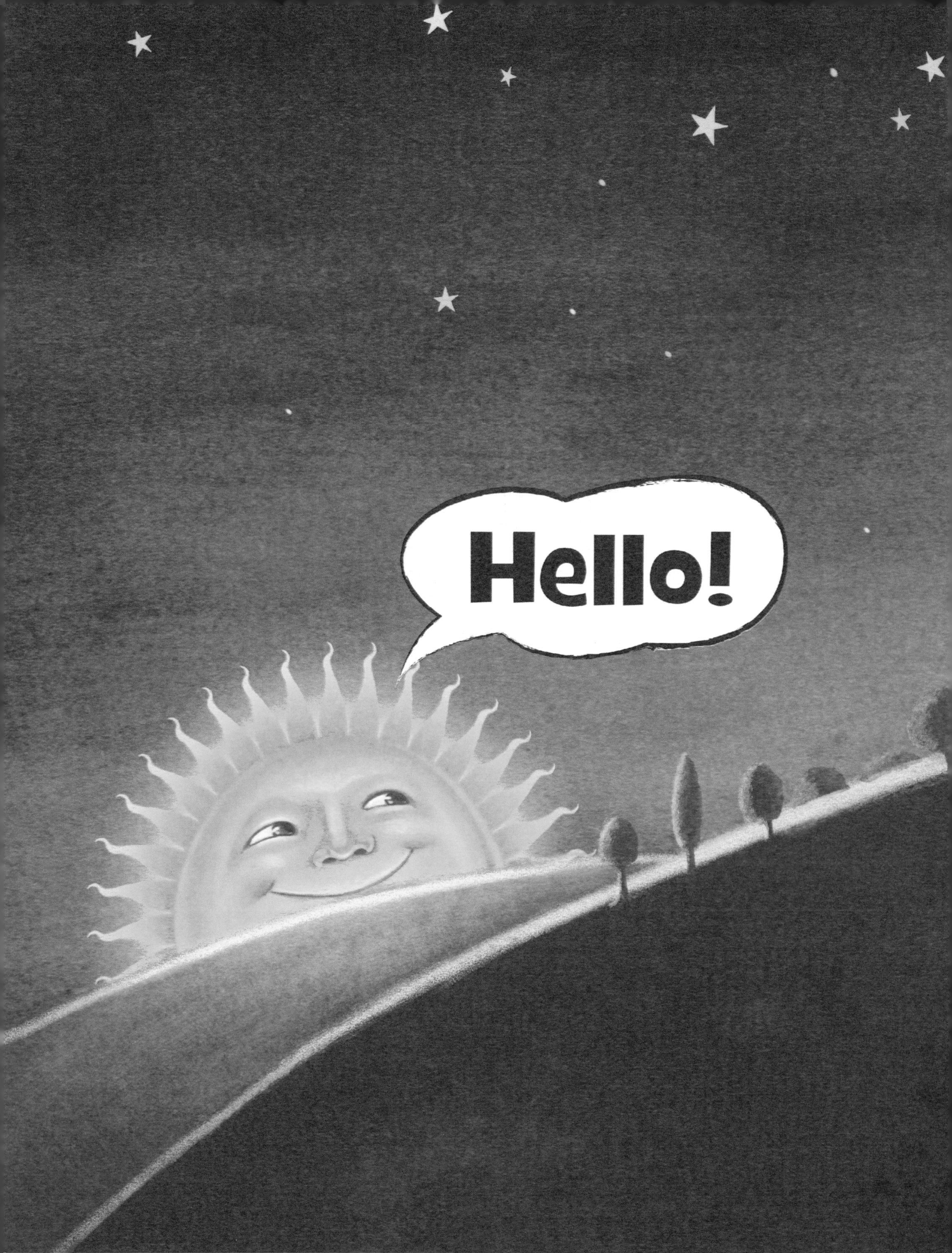
Hello!

and the light of the sun
will say "Hello" my friend!

But now my child
tucked in bed

be snug all night
while you sleep,
and while you slumber

you will keep safe

as you play in the Dream Time deep.

ABOUT THE AUTHOR:

James "Jim" West has been writing since 1998, inspired by the love for his beautiful hometown, Kent, Connecticut. The father of four incredible grown sons and two adorable grandchildren, he graduated from Stephen's College, Columbia, Missouri with a B.A. degree in healthcare and psychology and is a retired respiratory therapist. He taught Tai Chi and meditation classes in southwest Michigan for many years and currently resides on a lake in southeast Michigan where he continues to write full time. He also authored Swift The River Hoosie, a book of poetry and aphorisms, and will publish Where Katy Lives, an inspirational children's book, in late 2022.

ABOUT THE ILLUSTRATOR:

For 20+ years Anne has worked in the field of illustration and graphic design. During her carreer she worked for numerous publishers and has illustrated many children's books and book covers. She is also very active illustrating for the advertising industry, creating concepts for packaging and posters.

Anne lives with her family on the beautiful island of Maui, in Hawaii. She has a daughter, a son and a wonderful husband. She can be found often walking in nature with her husband and their black Labrador dog.

BOOKS WALKING THE WORLD

CPSIA information can be obtained
at www.ICGtesting.com
Printed in the USA
BVRC090901151021
619002BV00019B/128

* 9 7 8 1 7 3 4 3 9 1 2 2 0 *